What If a Lion Eats Me and I Fall into a Hippopotamus' Mud Hole?

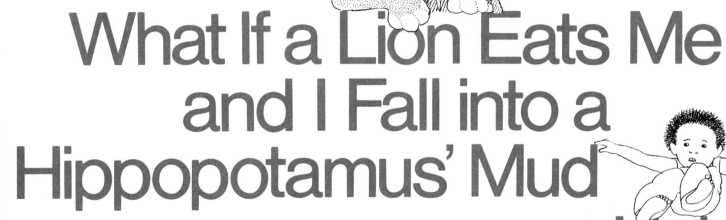

What If a Lion Eats Me and I Fall into a Hippopotamus' Mud Hole?

By **Emily Hanlon** / pictures by **Leigh Grant**

Delacorte Press / New York

To Ned, and with thanks to Peggy Parish—E. H.

For my family—L. G.

Text copyright © 1975 by Emily J. Tarasov
Illustrations copyright © 1975 by Leigh Grant

Manufactured in the United States of America

First printing

Typography by Lynn Braswell

Library of Congress Cataloging in Publication Data

Hanlon, Emily.
  What if a lion eats me and I fall into a hippopot-amus' mud hole?

  SUMMARY: Imagining all the possibilities for disaster that could happen at the zoo almost dissuades two friends from going.
  [1. Zoological gardens—Fiction.   2. Friendship—Fiction]   I. Grant, Leigh.   II. Title.
PZ7.H1964Wh   [E]   75-8007
ISBN 0-440-05950-X
ISBN 0-440-05951-8 lib. bdg.

U.S. 1879902

I have a friend named Stuart. I asked Stuart to go to the zoo with me.
But Stuart said, "No." He was afraid.
He had never been to the zoo before.

"What if the lion gets out of his cage?" asked Stuart. "He would eat me!"
"I have a magic dart gun," I told Stuart. "And if we see a lion out of its cage, I'll shoot it.

"The magic dart gun will put the lion to sleep. Then I'll drag the lion to its cage."

"But what if we meet a sea lion flip-flopping through the zoo?" Stuart asked. "The sea lion might want to bounce me in the air like a ball!"

"Then I'll bring a fish with us," I told Stuart. "If a sea lion starts bouncing you up in the air, I'll throw him a fish so he'll forget about you."
"But then I'll fall!" cried Stuart.

"Well," I told Stuart, "maybe there'll be an elephant strolling along and he'll catch you with his trunk."

"I don't think I'd like that," sighed Stuart.
"Elephants are very big...."
"But zoo elephants are very friendly," I told Stuart.
"And he would lift you up with his trunk and
put you in a tree—where you'd be safe.

"And there'd be some monkeys in the tree and they'd share their bananas with you."
Stuart smiled. "That might be fun." Then he frowned. "But how would I get down?"

"Why I'd go get the giraffe. She'd let
you slide down her neck;
and crawl across her back;
and swing down her tail!" I told Stuart.

"But what if I swing down into the lake?" cried Stuart. "And I wake up the crocodile and the alligator? And I can't swim!"

That would be a very dangerous situation,
I thought to myself. So I said to Stuart,
"Don't worry. I'd splash water in the
alligator's eyes so he couldn't see.
I'd get a stick and jump on top of the crocodile.
Then I'd ram the stick right between his jaws...
And then we'd hold onto our balloons...."

"I didn't know we had balloons," said Stuart.

"But we will," I promised him. "And we'll float out of the lake!"

"But what if a stork comes and pokes a hole in our balloons?" said Stuart. "And we fall into a hippopotamus' mud hole?

"And the mud is all yucchy? And we can't get our feet out of the mud?" cried Stuart.

"Well," I told Stuart. "I've been to
the zoo lots of times. And I know the
hippo very well. She won't hurt us.
If we're stuck in the mud,
she'll just open her mouth—
so we can hold onto her great big teeth—
and she'll pull us out of the mud.

"And then, because she's so friendly,
she'll probably let us climb on her back and give us a ride!"

"But what if it's dark by that time? And everyone else has gone home?
And we're left alone in the zoo?" asked Stuart. "And the wolves are howling?

"And the hyenas are laughing?

"And the lions and tigers are roaring?

"And the elephants are bellowing?"

That would be scary, I thought to myself. To be in the zoo, alone, at night. And what
if I couldn't do all those things: if the lion wanted to eat Stuart; if the sea lion wanted to bounce him;
if he fell into the lake or into the hippo's mud hole?

So I said to Stuart, "I guess today's not such a good day for the zoo."
Stuart looked surprised. "Are you afraid?" he asked.
How could I let Stuart know that I was afraid? So I said to him, "Of course not!"

And then I remembered something. "Stuart," I said, "what if
my daddy buys us a hot dog, popcorn, and ice cream?"
"Well..." said Stuart.

"I promise he will! He always does when we go to the zoo," I said.
"O.K.!" said Stuart. "Let's go!"

About the Author

EMILY HANLON was born in New York City and grew up in Westchester County, New York, where she now lives with her family. She attended the Dalton High School, and Barnard College, where she majored in English literature and writing. She married Ned Tarasov while still in college. When her two children, Nicky and Natasha, started school, Emily Hanlon began teaching retarded adults. When she realized that she really wanted to write, she stopped teaching to devote full time to children's books.

About the Artist

LEIGH GRANT grew up in Greenwich, Connecticut. She earned her B.A. at Hollins College in Virginia, her B.F.A. at Pratt Institute in Brooklyn, New York, and has studied in Europe at the Sorbonne. She has illustrated several books for children in England and the United States. Leigh Grant makes her home in Old Greenwich, Connecticut, where she spends her time illustrating children's books, horseback riding and raising finches.

About the Book

The illustrations were drawn with a Hunt's crow quill pen and FW ink on Strathmore two-ply plate finish paper. Leigh Grant likes to use the crow quill (a metal pen with a point shaped like a quill's, which must be hand dipped into the ink) because it delivers a very fine line and it is possible to make lines of varying widths with the single point. Many artists find the crow quill too slow and tedious, but Leigh Grant says it makes her feel like an artisan rather than a technician. The book has been set in Helvetica Light and Medium types by TypoGraphics Communications, Inc. It was printed by Rae Publishing and bound by A. Horowitz & Son.